The Candy-floss Tree

Three Poets

General Editor: Michael Harrison

The Candy-floss Tree

Gerda Mayer
Frank Flynn
Norman Nicholson

Oxford University Press
Oxford Toronto Melbourne

Oxford University Press, Walton Street, Oxford OX2 6DP

London Glasgow New York Toronto
Delhi Bombay Calcutta Madras Karachi
Nairobi Dar es Salaam Cape Town
Kuala Lumpur Singapore Hong Kong Tokyo
Melbourne Auckland

and associated companies in
Beirut Berlin Ibadan Mexico City Nicosia

Oxford is a trade mark of Oxford University Press

Three Poets
General Editor: Michael Harrison

British Library Cataloguing in Publication Data

Nicholson, Norman
The Candy-floss tree.   (Three poets)
1. Children's poetry, English
I. Title   II. Mayer, Gerda   III. Flynn, Frank
IV. Harrison, Michael, *1939–*
821'. 914'0809282   PZ8.3
ISBN 0-19-276053-X

The centre part of 'Three Autumns in
Regent's Park' is reproduced by
kind permission of Ceolfrith Press,
Sunderland Arts Centre.

Typeset by Rowland Phototypesetting Ltd,
Bury St Edmunds, Suffolk
Printed and bound in Great Britain by
Hazell Watson & Viney Limited,
Aylesbury, Bucks

Contents

GERDA MAYER

May Poem   7
Autumn   8
Bilberries   8
Poplar   9
Three Autumns in Regent's Park   10
A Lion, a Wolf and a Fox   11
Count Carrots   12
The Hansel and Gretel House   19
The Crunch   20

FRANK FLYNN

Yes   21
Swinging   22
Spaghetti   23
Clothes on the Washing Line   24
Puddle Splashing   25
Walking through the Park   26
Winter Morning   27
Foul Fowl   28
Seeing things   29
The Shed   30
Grandad's Teeth   31
But I Didn't   32
The Boy-eating Aspidistra   33

NORMAN NICHOLSON

Off to Outer Space Tomorrow Morning   35
Road Up   36
I Don't Believe in Ghosts   37
Ten Yards High   38

Five-inch Tall   40
In a Word   42
Turn on the Tap   43
Put on More Coal   45
The Man from the Advertising
        Department   46
Shepherds' Carol   47
Carol for the Last Christmas Eve   48

Gerda Mayer

May Poem

rain falls

the candy-floss tree
rains confetti and
bridesmaids

pink snowdrifts
lie on the path

First published in *Expression No. 7*, 1967

Autumn

summer, the shining one, is tarnished and rusted;
The sun-silvered leaves are corroded and fallen,
The shining hopes, little by little,
Dulled.
A small black wind
Angrily churns the leaves;
Autumn is on us;
Soon winter.

Bilberries

on the hillside
in shaggy coats
hobgoblin fruit
easy for little
hands

Poplar

propped up
against the pale
wall of the sky,
small birds
snipped from
black paper
pose there
in silhouette:
summer's dark plume is
winter's besom broom

Three Autumns in Regent's Park

The footballers
dance in the mist;
it muffles their shouts;
in muted colours
they rise
through the mist
through the trees.

        And once again
        the high stem of my heel
        roots in the damp
        leaf-mould for conkers –
        too late.

        Can't you remember –
        your father threw sticks for them
        and you carried them all off –
        years ago. . . .

Under a tree
St Francis
in an old mac
preaches sermons
to the birds
from a crumpled brown
paper bag.

A Lion, a Wolf and a Fox
Stoatley Rough, Haslemere, 1942–1944

I went to school in a forest where I was taught
By a lion, a wolf and a fox.
How the lion shone! As he paced across the sky
We grew brown-limbed in his warmth and among the
    green leaves.

The fox was a musician. O cunning magician you lured
A small stream from its course with your *Forellenlied,*
Teaching it Schubert; and made the children's voices
All sound like early morning and auguries for a fine day.

Now the wolf was a poet and somewhat grey and
    reserved,
Something of a lone wolf – thoughts were his pack;
There was a garden in that forest, walled with climbing
    roses,
Where we would sit or lie and hear the wolf recite.

And sometimes we would listen, and sometimes the
    voice
Would turn into sunlight on the wall or into a butterfly
Over the grass. It was the garden of poetry and so
Words would turn into flowers and trees into verse.

This morning I received the grey pelt of a wolf,
And the fox and the lion write they are growing old;
That forest lies many years back, but we were in luck
To pass through it then, that sunny and musical land.

Count Carrots

(from a Bohemian folk-tale called *Rübezahl*)

A small wind lightly
steps over the harebells. . . .

Like tall ragged kings
rise the fir trees of Bohemia. . . .

And I remember too
the scarlet and purple berries. . . .

He's the giant of the mountains;
they call him Count Carrots.
How he hates that nickname.
Let me tell you how he came by it.

Well – there was that princess
who – Persephone-like –
had strayed from her companions.
Perhaps you know the story.

It was all meadows and summer.
It was harebells and clover.
It was tall marguerites.
It was field flowers thousands and thousands,

or so it seemed.
The princess
was tempted to pick the best posy of all.
She ran this way and that, further and further away.

And the voices behind her grew fainter,
and the sky above her grew bluer,
and the sweet meadow engulfed her.
And suddenly – vast arms lifted her into the air.

The princess screamed. Or she may have fainted.
Then the giant of the mountain lifted her onto his
     shoulders.
He was swarthy and hairy; he was gnarled and muscled
     like trees.
His stride was long. The princess vanished from sight.

What had her companions been doing?
Asking the daisies who loved them.
Putting buttercups under each other's chin.
'If it shows gold in reflection, it means you like butter.'

Only later they missed her.
The consternation of it;
the runnings to and fro;
the calling, over and over.

'What shall we tell them at home?'
And who will comfort ever
the queen in tears,
the king in despair?

There was one other who heard the news
of the disappearance. He was the prince
whom the princess loved.
He saddled his horse and set out in search of her.

As for the giant, he carried the princess
to his cave under the mountains.
Some say he brought her gifts of precious stones
to tempt her to love him. This is untrue,

he was simpler than that. He brought her, I think,
bilberries from the forest, baskets of raspberries,
mushrooms, many sorts, which Bohemia excels in,
and clumsy importunings, day after day.

He brought her wild strawberries, gathered from steep
    hills.
She was used to sugar and cream; she was used to pretty
    bowls
from which to eat them. He roasted venison: the smoke
    stung her eyes, she said. She feared the spluttering fat.

The fact is – to paddle your feet in a mountain stream,
shallow and fast and cold as molten ice, water which
    rushes and swirls
over white pebbles, – to paddle your feet in this on a hot
    day
is pleasant and delightful: to wash in it, day after day,

indubitably cold. So the princess had discovered.
Besides, she missed her companions, she missed the
    court and the fun.
She missed, of course, her mother and father, she said.
She missed her little dog, Peep. And she missed her
    prince.

'Ah, giant, you brought me here against my
    inclinations.
I am not made for this rocky existence.
Forests are well enough for Sunday hikes.
My dog, Peep, would enjoy them.' Here her tears rolled
    down.

The giant, slow and ponderous, then had an idea,
which he should have thought of before.

He had some magic. He had a field of carrots.
He brought some to the princess. 'These carrots,' he said,

'can be changed, as you will, by magic into whomever,
whatever, you wish, say, your dog, Peep.'
So the princess wished, and one of the carrots
became her little dog. There he stood, yapping.

The princess, laughing in pleasure and disbelief,
stroked him and patted him and took him into her arms,
then put him down again; the little carrot dog
wagged his tail and sniffed at the venison. He was as like
    as like.

Then the princess went to work and said to one carrot:
'You'll be friend Sylvia.' And there Sylvia stood,
and laughed and embraced her, and was no carrot at all.
And so: 'You shall be Alice, you shall be John.'

Then the carrots were turned into friends and footmen,
chambermaids, courtiers, horses to ride on, by the
    princess, –
even goblets to drink from. Ah, but she had a good
    time.
She was gracious to the giant. She didn't see much of
    him.

She had a proper court. It was almost like home.
They went riding at dawn. In the evening they danced.
Then on the third morning, or was it the fourth?
her horse as she rode him began somewhat to droop.

A fine chestnut he was. What could be up with him?
He could hardly manage it back to the caves;
his step stumbling, his very flesh shrunken.
The princess was anxious and looked around for help.

'Sylvia', she cried to her friend, the groom not being
    around.
But Sylvia too looked pale and complained of her head.
Something was wrong with Sylvia. . . . Something was
    very wrong!
The groom she had called for lay in a ditch, dead,

and suddenly turned back into a carrot again.
Yes, carrots shrivel when out of the ground, and so
one by one as the carrots died so did her friends
shrivel and turn into carrots again – the magic gone.

That night at dinner only one servant was left to
pour out her wine. As he poured, he bent at the waist
more than he should. He drooped and tottered off;
and the stem of the wine-glass bent too. The wine spilt
    red.

Her face full of shock and woe, the princess went to the
    giant,
who looked guilty and sorry. But then he said:
'Darling princess, the fields are full of carrots.
I can bring you carrots freshly each day, to replace those
    lost.'

Well, so he did, but the princess felt uneasy;
until she hit on a cunning plan. 'Giant,' she pleaded,
'I fear you may one day run out of carrots. Count them
    for me
to see how many there are.' – So he did: one by one.

That would take him a day and a bit. His back was
    turned,
and he bent over the furrows with furrowed brow.
Then the princess picked some carrots, the freshest, the
    strongest,
and turned two into horses, and one into the prince,

the semblance of him whom she loved.
They rode away with the speed of a wish,
through forests of pine,
through thickets, past mountain streams,

into the valley below.
(Do not fear, do not falter,
do not yet fall behind.
Good Hope, stay by my side.)

So the princess prayed.
And they are fortunate
whom a vision of love
accompanies.

Meanwhile what of the giant?
Ah, but that booby
was still counting his carrots:
'Five-hundred . . . six-hundred . . .
    six-hundred-and-seventy-two. . . .

Did he try to pursue her?
The story says he did.
Surely, he lumbered one day out of the forest,
to knock her up, knock her down, rap for some
    reply. . . .

And no reply ever: the castle ears
closed tight to his bellowing lungs; the castle gates
forever shut to him; the curtains too,
though he reached to the topmost storey, drawn to his
    gaze.

Into the sulky night he plodded like thunder,
and the small pillow, rosy in lamplight, whispered
to the burly wind beating against the door:
'You will never bluster your way into *my* down.'

Henceforth, the giant was called Count Carrots by all;
a nickname he hates, as I told you at the beginning.
Woe to him who so calls him in mischief. Let the
impudent traveller, shouting his name, beware.

When I was small, I called his name to the forest:
'Count Carrots! Count Carrots!' then leapt into bed,
     half in fear.
He didn't come for me though. Could it be that perhaps
     he forgave me?
He loves children, they say. – May the forest stay green
     for him ever.

The Hansel and Gretel House

When you come across it
you'll know better than to
nibble.
Who's there? asks the witch.
The wind, cry the
startled children.

A house may look sweet
from outside: beware!
Things happen in pretty houses
you wouldn't believe. . . .

When the wind cries,
when the dog weeps,
when the voice of lost children
is heard in the wood,
let the forester hasten forth.

The Crunch

The lion and his tamer
They had a little tiff,
For the lion limped too lamely, –
The bars had bored him stiff.

No call to crack your whip, Sir!
Said the lion then irate:
No need to snap my head off,
Said the tamer – but too late.

Frank Flynn

Yes

Yes is a green word,
It grows like grass
It's as crinkly as cabbage,
It's as lush as lime
As springy as sprouts,
It's as lollopy as lettuce
As playful as peas
As artistic as apples.
Yes is as lazy as summer leaves
It's even as squelchy as a fist full of slime.

Swinging

Whenever I feel a little bit sad
I go on the swings in our local park.
At first I move backwards and forwards
Ever so slow
Closely studying the floor as I go,
Watching its cracks and its stones
Like I'm on a spaceship
Flying ever so low.
After a minute or two of swinging
I don't feel half so bad
Perhaps it's because space pilots never appear sad.
I press the accelerator into top gear;
Launch myself up at the sky
Until I get so high
Down is the only place left to go.
I zoom earthward like a meteor
Heading down from the sun,
Swing high, Swing low,
When you're down on a swing
Up is the only way you can go,
Swing low, Swing high.

Spaghetti

A plate heaped high
with spaghetti
all covered with tomato sauce
is just about my favourite meal.
It looks just like
a gigantic heap of:
steaming
        tangled
    mixed
        up
twizzled
        twisted
wound
    up
      woozled
WORMS!
I like picking them up
one at a time;
swallowing them slowly
head first,
until the tail flips
across my cheek
before finally wriggling
down my throat.
But best of all,
when I've finished eating
I go and look in a mirror
because the tomato sauce
smeared around my mouth
makes me look like a clown.

Clothes on the Washing Line

On windy days
mum puts the washing on the line;
I think it's fun to watch
as she hangs dad's shirts
upside down
and they wave their arms about
in a crazy sort of protest.
Mum's dresses always look
as though they're dancing,
but when I see my clothes
hanging on the line:
my favourite jeans
with patches on the knees,
my Liverpool football jersey
with a number seven on the back,
and a pair of grey football socks
that are supposed to be white,
it's like seeing bits of me
hanging there on the washing line.
I'm not really sure I like seeing
my clothes flapping in the wind,
I can't help feeling that I'm not altogether myself
and that I'm watching parts of me
waving me to join them.

Puddle Splashing

I'm fed up
with dry sunny days
because I've got this pair
of brilliant, bright, brand-new
yellow wellingtons
that shine like a new car
and come right up to my knee.
The next time it rains
I'm going puddle splashing
with my mate Jake.
Jumping from puddle to puddle
we'll make tidal waves,
or damming gutters with our boots
we'll turn streets into lakes,
while our laughter shakes raindrops
off the leaves of watching trees.

Walking through the park

After the Sunday morning rain
we go for an afternoon walk through the park.
The trees are heavy with a freshness
that drips from their leaves like syrup
on to the sleeve of my anorak.
I stick my fingers into the droplets,
licking their sweetness like lolly sticks.
Some way ahead
a small green caterpillar wriggles in space,
I look for the thread that attaches it
to the big branch above,
while the sun hangs suspended from the sky
like an aeroplane.
Dazzled by the sunlight
I don't manage to find the thread
but I don't mind,
I just continue walking through the park.

Winter Morning

On cold winter mornings
When my breath makes me think
I'm a kettle,
Dad and me wrap up warm
In scarves and Balaclavas,
Then we fill a paper bag
With bread and go and feed the ducks
In our local park.
The lake is usually quite frozen
So the ducks can't swim,
They skim across the ice instead,
Chasing the bits of bread
That we throw,
But when they try to peck the crumbs
The pieces slip and slide away.
Poor ducks!
They sometimes chase that bread
For ages and ages,
It makes me hungry just watching them,
So when dad isn't looking
I pop some bread in my mouth and have a quick chew.
The ducks don't seem to mind,
At least they've never said anything
To me if they do.

Foul Fowl

Mum says, 'Hens are fowl,'
I think they're a bit strange, but not quite that bad.
They stop in mid-step
with one leg stuck up in the air
as though they've forgotten how to walk.
When they want to look at you
they have to turn their heads so much to one side
I think they must have very poor eyesight;
my dad squints when he can't find his glasses
but even he doesn't have to turn his head completely
to one side when he wants to see something.
I feel sorry for hens,
apart from having poor eyesight
it must be difficult walking on your back legs
all the time.
I wonder what happened to their front legs?

Seeing Things

One day I said to Dad,
'Come and see this spider
'He's walking on air.'
Dad said,
'I must see this!'
And followed me into the garden.
'See!' I said, pointing to the spider
Who was moving while standing still.
Dad put on his glasses for a closer look,
Then he said, 'Your spider's not walking on
      air,
He's building a web
Spinning a thread,
He's a high wire walker
Making his wire as he walks,
Do you see?'
I nodded;
Dad seemed pleased and went indoors.
I didn't like to tell him
That although I could see what he had seen,
Dad hadn't seen the same thing as me:
I could see the spider hanging from a thread
Spinning a web with his eight legs weaving,
But when dad had gone
The thread and the web disappeared
As I faced the sun;
All that was left was
A spider with eight legs waving
To me
As he walked on air,
Which was really something worth seeing.

The Shed

There's a shed at the bottom of our garden
With a spider's web hanging across the door,
The hinges are rusty and creak in the wind.
When I'm in bed I lie and I listen,
I'll open that door one day.

There's a dusty old window around at the side
With three cracked panes of glass,
I often think there's someone staring at me
Each time that I pass,
I'll peep through that window one day.

My brother says there's a ghost in the shed
Who hides under the rotten floorboards,
And if I ever dare to set foot inside
He'll jump out and chop off my head,
But I'll take a peek one day.

I know that there isn't really a ghost,
My brother tells lies to keep the shed for his den;
There isn't anyone staring or making strange noises
And the spider has been gone from his web since I don't
    know when,
I'll go into that shed one day soon,

But not just yet. . . .

Grandad's Teeth

I thought that grandad was just an ordinary old man
Until he came to spend a holiday with us.
Early one morning before anyone else was awake
I crept into his bedroom
To see if he wanted to play war;
War games with grandad are always fun
Because he always lets me win,
But he was snoring,
Only his face bristling with grey grass
And with more cracks in it than dried mud
Peeked open-mouthed above the bedclothes.
He looked so old and tired that I decided
Our war could wait until after breakfast.
I was just about to leave
When I noticed something different about grandad's face:
His cheeks were hollow and his lips
Had all but disappeared.
I was just about to shout mum
To tell her that grandad was ill
When I noticed his teeth
In a glass of water
On a table
By his bed;
They were smiling at me
So I knew that grandad must be alright.
Later, when he came down to breakfast
The same teeth smiled at me again
But this time they were back in grandad's mouth.
Now, whenever he comes to stay
I wait until he's fast asleep
Then I sneak in and search his room
To see what other parts of his body
Grandad's taken off and hidden.

But I Didn't

When I got out of bed this morning
I might have tripped and fallen down
The stairs, breaking my neck as I did so,
    But I didn't,
Going to school
The bus might have crashed
In the morning rain
    But it didn't,
There might have been an earthquake
Causing the school to collapse
    before my maths test
    But there wasn't,
Eating school dinner
The fish might easily have been poisoned
Leaving me feeling dead
Instead of just sick, as usual,
    But it wasn't,
The sweet-shop I visited after school
Might have been robbed by men
With sawn-off shot-guns
Leaving me wounded
When I became a hero and tried to stop them
    But it wasn't,
I might have disturbed a burglar
When I got home
Instead of my mum taking a nap
    But I didn't,
Because I don't take chances
Nothing much happens to me
I'm careful never to walk on black lines
Between paving stones
And I always touch my nose and toes
Whenever I see an ambulance,
Being careful can be boring,
Tomorrow I might start taking chances
    But I won't.

The Boy-eating Aspidistra

My nan has got a plant
that she got from her nan,
she says one day it will belong to me,
but I'm not sure that I want it
cos I saw what it did to Dirty Dean Duggan.

Nan's plant is supposed to be an aspidistra,
it even looks a bit like one
with its dusty green leaves
spreading out from a pot
that looks like a giant pudding basin,
but I know nan's plant isn't quite what it seems
cos I saw what it did to Dirty Dean Duggan.

At my birthday party Dirty Dean
ate twelve cream cakes and four ice-creams,
I warned him that he would be sick
all over mum's best carpet,
Dean didn't take any notice,
instead he put some jelly down my back
then dumped the rest over nan's plant,
you can be sure I'd never do anything like that
cos I saw what it did to Dirty Dean Duggan.

As I cleaned the jelly off my back
I saw Dean eating his thirteenth cream cake,
unlucky for him!

A few minutes later his face went a funny shade of green;
he looked for somewhere to be sick where he wouldn't
    be seen,
then he rushed behind nan's aspidistra and stuck his
    head into the pot,
something I'd never dream of doing no matter how sick
    I felt
cos I saw what it did to Dirty Dean Duggan.

I was just about to tell mum what Dean had done
when I saw him disappearing head first
into nan's aspidistra,
he gave a muffled shout for help
but no one heard except me,
and I would never tell tales about nan's aspidistra
cos I saw what it did to Dirty Dean Duggan.

No one even noticed Dean's legs
kicking in the air as he disappeared from view,
until the only sign that he had ever been there at all
was a half-eaten cream bun lying on the floor,
nan's plant gave a loud burp,
which I thought rather rude,
but I didn't mention anything about manners
cos I saw what it did to Dirty Dean Duggan.

Afterwards there was the most terrible fuss,
I hear that the police are searching for Dean even now
but I didn't say a word about all that had happened
between Dean and nan's aspidistra
cos I saw what it did to Dirty Dean Duggan.

I knew people would never believe
what I said, and I wouldn't want
nan's aspidistra to be taken away,
cos I've written this list
of other rude boys I intend inviting for tea
with nan's aspidistra and me.

Norman Nicholson

Off to Outer Space Tomorrow Morning

You can start the Count Down, you can take a last look;
You can pass me my helmet from its plastic hook;
You can cross out my name in the telephone book –
     For I'm off to Outer Space tomorrow morning.

There won't be any calendar, there won't be any clock;
Daylight will be on the switch and winter under lock.
I'll doze when I'm sleepy and wake without a knock –
     For I'm off to Outer Space tomorrow morning.

I'll be writing no letters; I'll be posting no mail.
For with nobody to visit me and not a friend in hail,
In solit'ry confinement as complete as any gaol
     I'll be off to Outer Space tomorrow morning.

When my capsule door is sealed and my space-flight has begun,
With the teacups circling round me like the planets
    round the sun,
I'll be centre of my gravity, a universe of one,
     Setting off to Outer Space tomorrow morning.

You can watch on television and follow from afar,
Tracking through your telescope my upward shooting star,
But you needn't think I'll give a damn for you or what you are
     When I'm off to Outer Space tomorrow morning.

And when the rockets thrust me on my trans-galactic hop,
With twenty hundred light-years before the first stop,
Then you and every soul on earth can go and blow your top—
For I'm off to Outer Space tomorrow morning.

Road Up

What's wrong with the road?
Why all this hush? –
They've given an anaesthetic
In the lunch-hour rush.

They've shaved off the tarmac
With a pneumatic drill,
And bandaged the traffic
To a dead standstill.

Surgeons in shirt-sleeves
Bend over the patient,
Intent on a major
Operation.

Don't dare sneeze!
Don't dare shout!
The road is having
Its appendix out.

I Don't Believe in Ghosts

I don't believe in ghosts.
       No matter how they talk
Of an old man with whiskers
       White as chalk,

Who sits beside a window
       Above the dark yards,
Dealing a round
       Of invisible cards.

Go in if you want to!
       Creep up the stairs,
Build a makeshift table
       Of two broken chairs;

Switch on your pocket torch;
       Play three-handed rummy,
With one empty place
       And no one for dummy;

Hold back your aces;
       Don't try to win.
See if the old joker
       Will want to join in.

You'll deal yourself a blank hand!
       Never you fear!
I don't believe in ghosts –
       But I'm staying here.

Ten Yards High

I'm ten yards high.
The jackdaws fly
Out from the chimney-pots
As I stride by.
'Clumsy clown!'
The mothers cry
When I push down the washing
With the jut of my thigh.
'Look where you put
Your foot!' – but I
Don't give a hoot
If the line is in a tangle
Or the sheets are apple-pie.
Let them hang their clothes to dry
Out of reach of my boot.
For they're quite beneath my notice
From this window-sill, skylight,
Roof-line height.
When the weather's chill
Smoke from fires
Brings tears to my eye,
And if I stand still
The sparrows fight
To shelter in the eaves
Of my collar and tie.
I peep in dormer-casements,
See beds unmade
And tights flung awry –
The girls draw the curtains
As I creep by!
I bend down and pry
Into upper flights
Of double-deck buses,

Get an eyeful of the trouble
The conductor misses;
Stare straight in the face
Of the Town Hall Clock;
Strike a match on the roof
Of the Market block;
Bump into the church,
Hold tight to the spire,
Look down on the churchyard
Where one day I'll lie
In a grave as long
As a cokernut shy.
And when I die
Will the sextons all
Knock off and down spades
At the sight of my
Unburied length?
Will they call it a day
And demand extra pay?
And will everyone say:
'He was a man
Of such power and strength
He could toss that tower
Right up to the sky.
Oh, he'll be a hero
A thousand years!
And the reason why? –
He was ten yards high.'

Five-inch Tall

I'm five-inch tall.
I dive and crawl
Into the jungle
Of the uncut lawn.
Fawn-coloured stems
Of plate-size daisies
Sway round my head
In a tangle of weed.
A monstrous, pop-eyed,
Dinosaur snail
Stares out from the dome
Of his mobile home,
Leaving a slime-trail
Wide as a drain.
In distant, dark-furred
Thickets of twitch,
A cricket whirs
Like a motor-mower.

I creep from the lower
Foothills of lawn
Into a conifer
Forest of horse-tails,
Where writhing, boa-
constrictor worms
Coil round fern-trunks
Or heave through the soil.

Undaunted, unshaken,
I break from the shade
To a lake of sunlight –
Five-inch tall
And the heir of acres,
With all the walled dukedom
To call my own.

But high on a pear-tree
A pocket falcon,
With bragging, flaunted,
Red-flag breast,
Is poised to strike;
Dives down and pounces –
Grappling-iron talons
And beak like a pike.
Shaken, daunted,
Arms over my chest,
I cringe and turn tail;
Off like a shot
To the vegetable plot,
Helter-skelter for the shelter
Of broccoli and kale;
Yielding the field
To red-rag robin –
For safety is all
When you're five-inch tall.

In a Word

Sun –
       In a word –
              beams
Rain –
       A green bird –
              drops
Snow –
       White and furred –
              flakes
Thunder –
       All heard –
              claps
Applause, applause, applause,
       Because
Something's always happening
       In a word.

Turn on the Tap

Turn on the tap!
See a waterfall
Spout from the pipe:
A thin rill
That spills down a gill
Where salmon shoot
The rapids upward,
Fins clinging
To rock-crack and root.
See cool drops drool
From an upland pool,
Where rice-grain bubbles
Ooze through the mud,
And the silt stirs
In the troubled current
Clogging the stems
Of bog-bean and rush.
Neither willow nor alder
Breaks the bare shore;
But the still lake-water
Reflects the black
Jag-edge of crag,
The tumbled cap
Of the summit cairn –
Turn on the tap:
You're drinking a tarn.

Turn on the tap!
Hear the west wind
Howl up from Ireland,
Skimming the scum
Off the simmering seas.
Keep your ears skinned
For the whistling kettle
Of the hot Atlantic,
For the rattle of hail
Like a clout of dried peas
Flung on a drum.
The oceans steam
In the sun's sweaty breath;
Mist-wreaths settle
On every humped hill;
As huge sponges of clouds
Wring themselves out
Into pot-hole and spout.
England's long backbone
Is drenched to the marrow,
As the funnels of storm
Pour down on the fells
And swill into narrow
Channels and runnels
Of ditch and drain –
Turn on the tap:
You're drinking rain!

Put on More Coal

Put on more coal!
See ferrets of fire
Glide through the age-old
Forest glades;
See horse-tails higher
Than a chimney stack
Spire up and crash
Down cindery screes;
See an up-the-flue draught
Breeze round the boles
Of fossilized ferns,
Turning the ash
Bonfire-bright.
Put on more coal:
You're burning trees!

Put on more coal!
See caves of rubble
Bubble and crack
Under weight of flame;
See long-dead miners,
Bare-backed and black,
Turn in their graves,
Awake to work again,
And ram at the rock
In the pit of the night.
Stir up the fire!
Each hundredweight won
From a fight with the dark.
Put on more coal:
You're burning men!

The Man from the Advertising Department

There's more to see
In the next field.
Not much here
But grass and daisies
And a gulley that lazes
Its way to the weir –
Oh there's much more to see
In the next field.

There are better folk
In the next street.
Nobody here
But much-of-a-muchness people:
The butcher, the blacksmith,
The auctioneer,
The man who mends the weathercock
When the lightning strikes the steeple –
But they're altogether a better class
In the next street.

There'll be more to do
In the next world.
Nothing here
But breathing fresh air,
Loving, shoving, moving around a bit,
Counting birthdays, forgetting them, giving
Your own little push to the spin of the earth;
It all amounts to
No more than living –
But by all accounts
There'll be more to do
And more to see
And V.I.P. neighbours
In the next world.

Shepherds' Carol

Three practical farmers from back of the dale —
      Under the high sky —
On a Saturday night said 'So-long' to their sheep
That were bottom of dyke and fast asleep —
      When the stars came out in the Christmas sky.

They called at the pub for a gill of ale —
      Under the high sky —
And they found in the stable, stacked with the corn,
The latest arrival, newly-born —
      When the stars came out in the Christmas sky.

They forgot their drink, they rubbed their eyes —
      Under the high sky —
They were tough as leather and ripe as a cheese
But they dropped like a ten-year-old down on their
    knees —
      When the stars came out in the Christmas sky.

They ran out in the yard to swap their news —
      Under the high sky —
They pulled off their caps and roused a cheer
To greet a spring lamb before New Year —
      When the stars came out in the Christmas sky.

Carol for the Last Christmas Eve

The first night, the first night,
     The night that Christ was born,
His mother looked in his eyes and saw
     Her maker in her son.

The twelfth night, the twelfth night,
     After Christ was born,
The Wise Men found the child and knew
     Their search had just begun.

Eleven thousand, two fifty nights,
     After Christ was born,
A dead man hung in the child's light
     And the sun went down at noon.

Six hundred thousand or thereabout nights,
     After Christ was born,
I look at you and you look at me
But the sky is too dark for us to see
     And the world waits for the sun.

But the last night, the last night,
     Since ever Christ was born,
What his mother knew will be known again,
And what was found by the Three Wise Men,
And the sun will rise and so may we,
     On the last morn, on Christmas Morn,
Umpteen hundred and eternity.